Little Kitty

by Lauryne Hope

Illustrations by Raynald Kudemus

To order additional copies of this book, contact:
Xlibris
844-714-8691
www.Xlibris.com
Orders@Xlibris.com

ISBN: Softcover   978-1-4771-3097-1
         EBook   978-1-4771-3098-8

Print information available on the last page

Rev. date: 08/27/2020

Dedicated to
Katherine and Frederick

Little Kitty in the tree
Won't you come and play with me?
You can climb another day
If you have to get away.

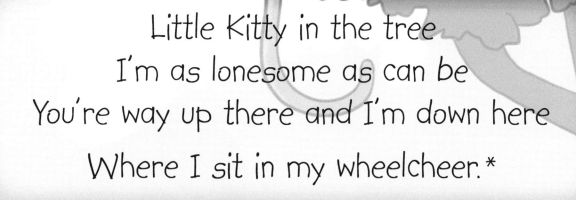

Little Kitty in the tree
I'm as lonesome as can be
You're way up there and I'm down here

Where I sit in my wheelcheer.*

*wheelchair

I cannot jump, I cannot climb
I hope I can, ahead in time.
You look so lost, you need a friend,
Come play with me until day's end.

Kitty, Kitty, come on down,
Let's change our faces from a frown.
Why, look you're lower on the branch,
That must be I'll have a chance.

I'll show you that I'll love you
Give you milk, throughout the day
Pet you when you're tired,
And at the end of play.

Oh, now I'm happy as can be
Here you are to play with me.
First up here, sit on my lap
So I can pat you on the nap.*

*nape

Your coat is soft and silky
Your purring is divine.
I'm glad you came to see me,
Now you can be mine.

The End

Printed in the United States
By Bookmasters